CARTOON NETWORK

SCOOBY-DOO! and the HALLOWEEN HOTEL HAUNT

A GLOW IN THE DARK Mystery!

By Jesse Leon McCann

ISBN 0-439-11768-2

12 11 10 9 8 7 6 5 4 3 2 1 9/9 0 1 2 3 4/0

Design by Peter Koblish • Printed in the Singapore • First Scholastic printing, October 1999

SCHOLASTIC INC.
New York Toronto London Auckland Sydney Mexico City New Delhi Hong Kong

THE PRIMM HOTEL

Scooby-Doo and his friends from Mystery, Inc. were invited to a Halloween costume party at a fancy hotel. But when they arrived, all of the party guests were running outside. They looked very frightened.

Daphne spotted Ms. Primm. She was the nice woman who owned the hotel.

"What's the matter?" Daphne asked. "Why is everyone running away?"

"Oh, it's terrible! Just terrible!" cried Ms. Primm. "Some of the guests spotted a real phantom in the hotel! It's too scary!"

"Looks like we've got a new mystery to solve!" said Fred.

Velma pointed to one of the hotel's windows. "And I think I see what frightened everyone," she said. "Look!"

What did Velma see?

Turn off the lights and you'll see it, too!

Do you think this is what scared the party guests?

Fred, Daphne, Velma, Shaggy, and Scooby went inside The Primm Hotel to investigate. They were met by Seymour Primm. He was the hotel manager and Ms. Primm's nephew.

"This is awful!" Seymour cried. "We'll have to sell the hotel now. No one will want to stay here if it's haunted!"

"Like, who could blame them?" Shaggy agreed. "The spook could be anywhere!"

"Reah, anywhere!" Scooby agreed.

"Don't worry, Seymour," Fred told him. "We'll get to the bottom of this mystery. If there's a phantom in this hotel, we'll find it!"

Daphne looked around. "Yes, but where do we start?" she asked. "This is an awfully big hotel."

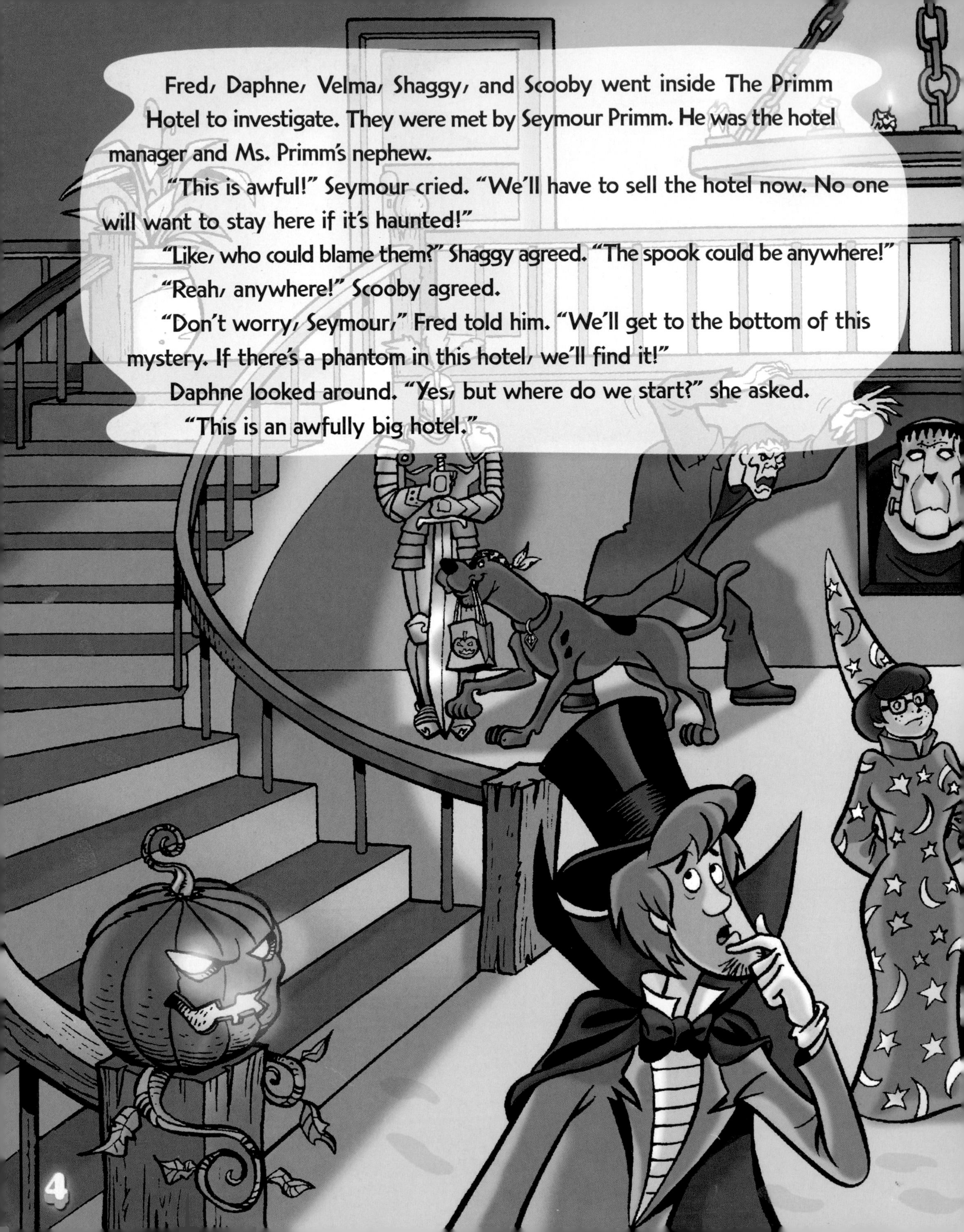

OFFICE
You can help the gang get started!
Turn off the lights to see which way the gang should go.
Where do you think the phantom was headed? Where do you think the phantom came from?

Scooby and his friends went up the stairs to the second floor. They walked quietly down the hallway, looking for clues. It was dark, silent, and a little spooky.

Suddenly, there was a loud noise. *CREEEEAK!*

Scooby leaped into Shaggy's arms. "Roh, no! The rhantom!" Scooby yelped.

"Relax, Scooby," Velma said. "It was probably just a creaky floorboard. This hotel is pretty old, you know."

"Zoinks!" said Shaggy. "Like, this hallway is giving me the creeps! I feel like someone is watching us."

Scooby nodded his head. "Reah, re too!" he agreed.

"I'm sure no one is watching us," Daphne said. "You two chickens are just letting your imaginations get the better of you."

Was Daphne right?

Turn out the lights and see!

Who is it? What do you think caused the loud noise?

"We'll search farther down the hall," Fred said. "Shaggy, you and Scooby check this room."

Fred pointed into a dark, eerie room. Shaggy and Scooby shook their heads from side to side.

"Like, no way, Fred! Scoob and I are not going to snoop around a scary, run-down hotel room!" Shaggy said. "But we'll be glad to 'run down' and wait in the van. Right, Scooby?"

"Right!" agreed Scooby.

Velma promised Shaggy and Scooby some Scooby Snacks and an extra Halloween treat bag if they would search the room. What's a chowhound to 'doo? Scooby caved.

As quietly as they could, Scooby and Shaggy tiptoed through the room. Shaggy noticed a big door and opened it. When they saw what was inside they screamed and jumped into the laundry chute!

Shaggy and Scooby-Doo slid down, down, DOWN the long laundry chute. They yelled the whole way down.

KA-THUNK! At the bottom of the chute, they landed in a laundry basket and tipped it over. They were in the hotel's laundry room, where all the guests' linens and bath towels were washed and dried.

They jumped up and ran to a corner of the room far away from the chute. No phantom was going to land on them.

Suddenly, Shaggy let out a scream and waved his arms through the air.

"Help! Help! Like, the phantom's touching me!" Shaggy cried.

"Re too! Re too!" Scooby howled. "Relp!"

Now both Shaggy and Scooby were clawing at the air around them, trying to push the phantom away. They couldn't see the phantom, but they felt it tickling them from above!

What did Shaggy and Scooby really feel?
Switch off the lights and check it out!
What was tickling Shaggy and Scooby? Would it fool you too?

What jumped out at Velma?
Shut off the lights and see — if you're *not* too scared!
Were you surprised like Velma was? What should the gang do now?

Fred, Daphne, and Velma heard Shaggy and Scooby screaming in the basement.

"Come on, gang! Let's go back downstairs," Fred told Daphne and Velma. "It sounds like Shaggy and Scooby are in trouble!"

They ran back down the old staircase to the first floor as fast as they could.

THUMP! There was a strange noise coming from the grand ballroom. Velma, Daphne, and Fred went in to investigate. The grand ballroom was all decked out for the Halloween costume party and looking very cool.

Daphne looked around. "Well, Shaggy and Scooby aren't in here," she said. "I'm surprised. There's so much food!"

"Nope, no one here but these fake monsters," Velma said as she looked behind one of the phony paper ghouls. "I don't think these could scare anyone.

"AAAAH!" Velma jumped back in fear.

Something leaped out from behind the paper monster and moaned eerily.

Meanwhile, Shaggy and Scooby-Doo were running through a spooky service corridor deep underneath the hotel. They still thought the phantom was after them. They could feel something touching their feet and ankles.

"Like, the phantom is trying to grab us, Scoob!" Shaggy yelled. "Run for your life!"

"Relp! The rhantom's got re!" Scooby cried.

They tried to run without touching the ground. They ran so fast and so far, they didn't even notice that the corridor had ended, and they ran right into an underground cave. It didn't matter, though. They could still feel slimy, creepy things touching their feet. Shaggy and Scooby just wanted to get away!

What do you think was touching them?
Click off the lights and find out.
Was it the phantom? What was it?

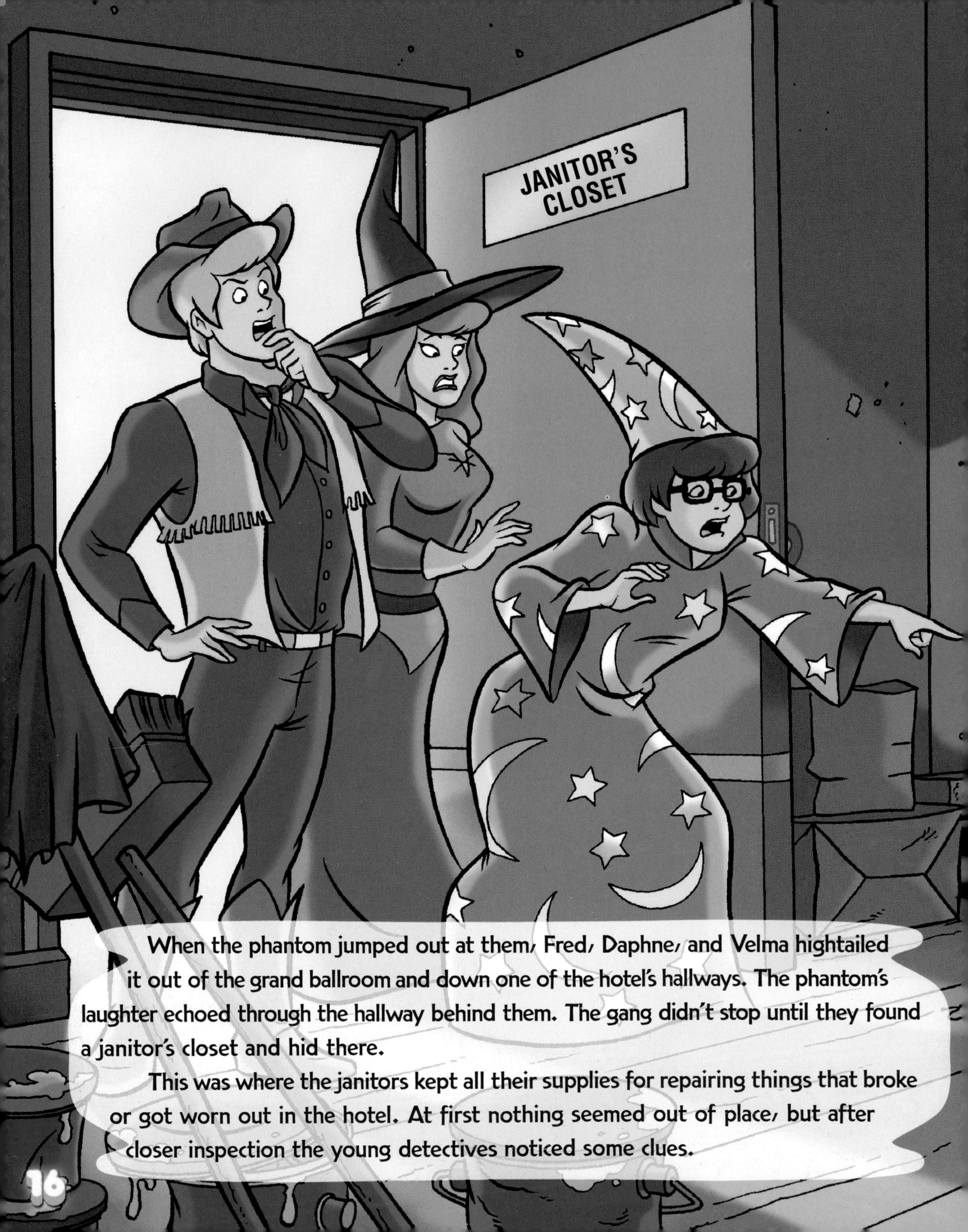

When the phantom jumped out at them, Fred, Daphne, and Velma hightailed it out of the grand ballroom and down one of the hotel's hallways. The phantom's laughter echoed through the hallway behind them. The gang didn't stop until they found a janitor's closet and hid there.

This was where the janitors kept all their supplies for repairing things that broke or got worn out in the hotel. At first nothing seemed out of place, but after closer inspection the young detectives noticed some clues.

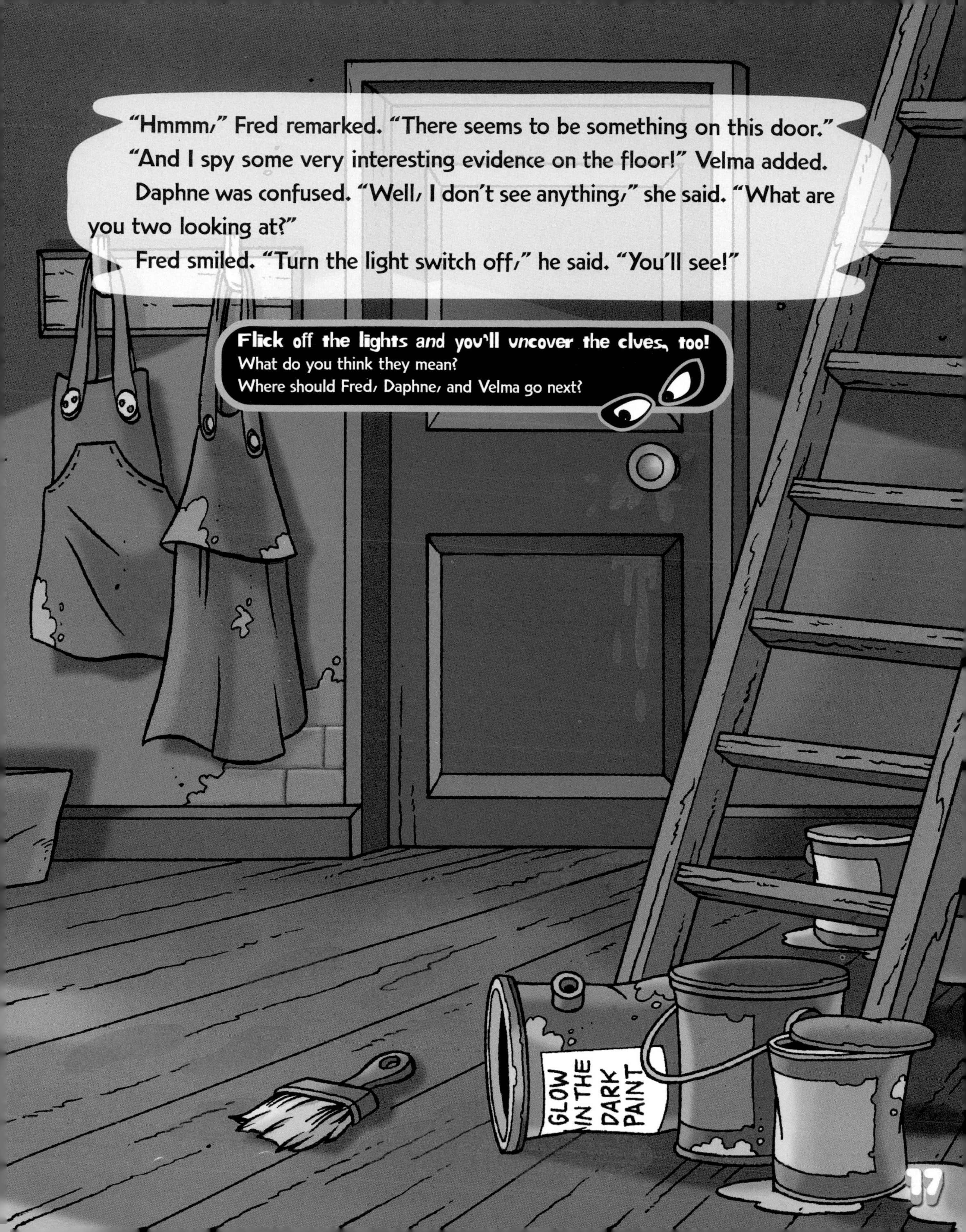

"Hmmm," Fred remarked. "There seems to be something on this door."

"And I spy some very interesting evidence on the floor!" Velma added.

Daphne was confused. "Well, I don't see anything," she said. "What are you two looking at?"

Fred smiled. "Turn the light switch off," he said. "You'll see!"

Flick off the lights and you'll uncover the clues, too!
What do you think they mean?
Where should Fred, Daphne, and Velma go next?

"Help! Help!" cried Shaggy. "This phantom won't give up!"

"Roooh-oh-oh!" Scooby yelped.

Now they were deep inside the underground cave. All around them was mining equipment — the kind miners use when they're digging for gold.

Scooby-Doo and Shaggy tried to hide from the phantom. They thought the phantom was whirling around in the air above their heads. They could hear the fluttering of wings and a strange noise that went, "TWEE! TWEE!"

"Like, I think we're goners, Scooby!" Shaggy shouted as he ducked down. "Goners!"

Scooby ducked, too, and covered his head. "Reah, roners," he agreed.

What was really flying over Shaggy's and Scooby's heads?
Turn out the lights and look for yourself.
What do you see?

Shaggy and Scooby hid under one of the mining machines. Suddenly Shaggy realized something.

"Hey, Scoob," Shaggy said, smiling. "That wasn't the phantom. It was only bats! And, like, now that I think of it, that wasn't the phantom in the hallway or the laundry room, either. It was just spiderwebs and bugs and snakes we felt! Pretty silly, huh?"

"Ree-hee-hee, right!" Scooby laughed. "Rilly!"

Then Shaggy and Scooby noticed the digging and mining machines in the cave. It was very strange. But they saw something stranger. Two men were on the other side of the cave talking to someone who wasn't there!

Shaggy and Scooby started to sneak back up to the hotel without being seen by the two men. CRASH! Scooby and Shaggy bumped right into Fred, Daphne, and Velma. Before he could help himself, Scooby let out a big "RELP!"

Instantly, the two men turned toward the kids.

"Get them!" cried a third voice that seemed to come from nowhere.

Who were the two men talking to? Who called out?
Turn the lights out and check!
Who do you think the men are?
Do you think Scooby and the gang will get caught?

"Come on, gang!" Fred shouted. "Back up to the ballroom! Hurry!"

Fred, Velma, Daphne, Shaggy, and Scooby-Doo ran out of the cave and up to the ballroom as fast as they could. They quickly ducked into a corner to hide.

"I wonder what happened to the phantom?" Daphne asked.

"Like, I think the phantom is the least of our troubles," whispered Shaggy. "Those two goons don't look very friendly."

The two mysterious miners were getting closer.

"You're right, Shaggy," Velma agreed. "I bet they're up to something shady."

"Don't worry, gang! Before we ran into Shag and Scoob, I had a chance to set a trap for the phantom," Fred told them. "The trap will work just as well on these two."

What trap is Fred talking about?
Where is the phantom?
Dim the lights and sneak a peek!
Will the trap work? Who will get caught in it?

Fred released a net that caught the two men — and the phantom! Fred pulled off the phantom's mask. It was Seymour Primm!

"There's an old gold mine under the hotel," said Seymour angrily. "I thought if I scared everyone away, my aunt would sell the hotel to the miners and I'd be rich. But I didn't count on these meddling kids and their pesky dog!"

"Thank you," said Ms. Primm to the gang. "Here's a reward."

"Like, where?" asked Shaggy. "I don't see anything!"

But Scooby-Doo knew there was something on the tray. He dimmed the lights and he was right! SCOOBY-DOOBY-DOO!

And if you dim the lights, you'll see the glow-in-the-dark reward, too!